Hostage

Malorie Blackman

With illustrations by
Derek Brazell

For Neil and Elizabeth, with love

First published in 2002 in Great Britain by
Barrington Stoke Ltd
18 Walker Street, Edinburgh, EH3 7LP

www.barringtonstoke.co.uk

This edition first published 2013

First published in *Amazing Adventure Stories* edited by Tony Bradman
(Transworld, 1994)

4u2read edition based on *Hostage*, published by Barrington Stoke, 1999

ISBN: 978-1-78112-249-5

Printed in China by Leo

Contents

Chapter 1
Kidnap

When I came out of school, it was dark. I zipped my jacket right up to my chin. I didn't know what to do next. I wasn't going back to our house, that was for sure.

I made up my mind to go to the High Street for an ice-cream and then maybe go and see a film. That way I could put off seeing Dad. I didn't want to see him at all – not after the row we'd had that morning before I left for school.

I hated our house, I never called it home. Not now that Mum had gone. It always felt so empty. And Dad and I never seemed to have much to say to each other.

I dug into my pockets and found two safety pins, a pencil, some gum and a few other things – but not much money. So I couldn't go to a film. But an ice-cream, yes!

"Angela?"

I turned when I heard my name. A woman with short, brown hair smiled at me from a blue car.

I'd never seen her before, so how did she know my name?

I stood still.

"Angela?" she said again.

"Yeah?" I replied.

Then I felt a warm, smelly hand over my mouth and a strong arm around my waist. Before I could even blink, I was lifted off my feet.

A man said something behind me, but I couldn't hear what it was. My heart thumped. I was pushed into the car. No time to kick or shout. The car raced off down the road.

Chapter 2
Blind Panic

It had been so quick.

I looked around me. A blond man in a grey raincoat sat on my right. A bald man in a blue jacket sat on my left. I was jammed in between them.

I was so scared that I opened my mouth and yelled, as loud as I could. At once the bald guy put his hand over my mouth.

"SHUT UP!" he hissed at me.

His fingers smelt of petrol. I tried to yell through his fingers but it made me choke.

"We're not going to hurt you, do you hear?" said Baldy. "We just want to make sure your dad does what we tell him to do. As soon as he does, we'll let you go. Understand?"

I didn't say anything. I *couldn't*. If I opened my mouth I'd be sick.

"Don't yell again, or else ..." said the blond man. Baldy took his hand away from my mouth. I opened it to yell again. At once Baldy's hand was back over my mouth.

"If that's the way you want it," he said, in an angry voice.

The hand he held over my mouth and nose was pressing down so hard that it hurt. I couldn't breathe. I pulled at his fingers with

both of my hands but he just pressed down
harder. I looked up at him. I was crying. He
moved his hand a little way from my mouth. I
gulped in some air. I wanted to shout and throw
myself at the car door.

I kept telling myself, don't panic ... I must
think ... I must make a plan.

"That's better, Angela," said Baldy in a low voice. "Keep still and do as we say and we'll all be better off."

"In more ways than one!" laughed the blond man. His evil laugh scared me.

I looked out of the windows. I was going to throw myself at one of the car doors and hope someone would see me. But the driver knew Deansea very well. She kept to the back streets where there was no one around and no traffic lights to make the car stop.

What should I do?

Baldy had said Dad must do what they wanted. Was that why they'd grabbed me? It had to be that. When Dad left the army he took over the best jewellery shop in Deansea. He was glad that children didn't come into jewellery shops. Dad didn't like children.

The car went over a bump and I stopped thinking about Dad. *I must do something!*

We left Deansea by the old church road.

"Tie a scarf over her eyes," the woman told the blond man.

"Do we have to do that?" said Baldy with a frown. "We'll be gone before they find her. Does it matter if she sees where we go?"

"Do as I say," the woman ordered in an angry voice.

"No! NO!" I yelled.

I was not going to let them tie that scarf over my eyes without a fight. I kicked and hit out as hard as I could. Baldy grabbed me by the arms. The blond man tried to get the scarf over my eyes. When one of his hands came near my mouth I bit it – *hard*. He swore. Then he shook me hard.

"Do that again and I'll make sure your dad never sees you again. Do you understand?" he hissed.

I said nothing.

"UNDERSTAND?" he shouted.

I nodded. I was scared.

"Good. Now keep still," he said.

I couldn't move. I remembered how I didn't want to go home after school because I didn't want to see Dad. Now I might *never* see him again.

Chapter 3
Countdown

They wanted Dad's jewels – that was it. But would Dad hand over the jewels just for me? After our row that morning, I wasn't sure that he would. Ever since Mum left, Dad and I were always having rows.

'Don't panic,' I told myself. 'You're not dead yet.'

But it was hard. My heart was thumping and I felt sick.

I had to work out where I was. I tried to see out from under the scarf. No good. Now what?

Well … we'd gone down the old church road. Then after they tied the scarf over my eyes, we'd gone on for three or so minutes more. How fast? Not as fast as Dad when he drove, so less than 40 miles an hour? I wasn't sure.

I started to count. When I got to 600, the car turned left. I started from one again. I was counting out the seconds. It was a trick Dad knew from the army. The only time we didn't row was when he told me stories about his time in the army.

I went on counting. The car didn't turn off that road until I got to 1,400. Then it turned right. I counted to 120 before the car turned right again. Then we must have gone down a track or over a field because we bumped around a lot.

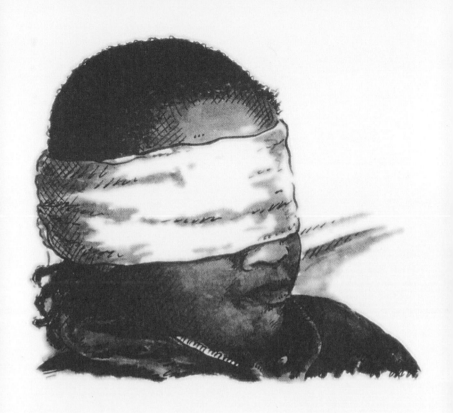

And all the time, no one in the car said a word. 600 left, 1,400 right, 120 right. Could I remember that?

Then the car stopped and the engine was turned off. The car doors opened. I sat still, while the others got out of the car.

"This way," the woman said.

Someone grabbed my arm and pulled me out of the car. The snow crunched under my feet. I heard the sound of the wind in the trees. We started to walk. After ten steps the ground became hard. We had gone into a house. A door shut behind me. I was very, very scared.

After five steps, Baldy said, "We're going up some stairs!"

There were 12 steps up.

At the top of the stairs I was led into a room. I stood still.

"C-Can I t-take the scarf off n-now?" I said in a low voice.

No one stopped me as I pulled off the scarf. I blinked in the light. The room was dark and dirty. It was empty apart from a chair and a table with a newspaper on it. The window had planks of wood nailed across it. No one said a word.

"W-What do you want my dad to do?" I asked.

After all, I was still alive. I could find a way out of this. I knew I could.

The two men smiled at each other.

"Let's just say, we want him to come up with the goods," said the blond man.

"And he'd better not mess us about," said Baldy.

"Come up with the goods ...?" I said in a shaky voice.

"Yeah!" Baldy grinned. "We want ..."

"Shut up, Quill!" the blond man snapped.

So now I knew the bald guy's name.

"No names in front of the girl – remember?" the woman hissed.

They all turned to look at me. I couldn't help it – I began to cry. Dad wouldn't cry if he was here, I told myself. Nothing could ever make Dad cry.

"Tie her up," said the woman.

"I'll do it," said Quill.

Could I make a break for it? I could get past the two men, but the woman was right by the door.

Then the woman walked over to Quill and said something in his ear.

Now was the time to get away.

But Quill moved forward to stand in front of me. I had lost my chance. Would I get another?

Chapter 4
Held to Ransom

"When you've tied her up, come downstairs," said the woman. "I want to talk to you – *both* of you."

The woman and the blond man left the room. I heard them going down the stairs.

"Don't tie me up, Quill," I begged in a soft voice. "I'd hate that."

"I've got to tie you up," Quill said. "And don't call me Quill in front of the others."

I shook my head. I wasn't that stupid.

"Are you ... after the jewels in Dad's shop? Are those the goods you want him to hand over?" I asked.

Quill took some thin rope out of his pocket and nodded. My heart sank. Dad used the same kind of rope for tying up parcels at home. It was thin but very strong, too strong to break.

"Once we get the jewels, we'll let you go," said Quill.

"And if Dad won't hand them over?"

"He wants you back, doesn't he?"

That was the problem. *I didn't know*. Dad loved his shop and his jewels. Dad had always gone off to his shop when the rows between

him and Mum got too bad. Sometimes I thought he loved his jewels more than me. Then I felt silly and angry. How could I get so upset that he spent so much time with his bits of metal and fancy glass?

"Come on. This won't take long. Put your hands behind your back," Quill ordered.

Slowly I did as I was told. Then I remembered something Dad had told me. He'd learnt how to do it in the army.

When Quill tied up my wrists, I kept them together and bent my hands back. When he tied up my ankles, I kept them together and twisted my feet apart. Dad told me that if you did this, the rope is not tied as tight.

Quill tied the rope and stood up. "Do I have to gag you?" he asked.

I shook my head. I hated the thought of anything over my mouth.

"One single sound out of you and I'll muzzle you like a dog."

I nodded.

"It's no good shouting or yelling. There's no one for miles around. All you'll do is make the two down below very angry with you. Do you understand?" Quill said.

I nodded again. I heard footsteps, then the other two came back into the room. The woman was talking to Dad on a mobile phone.

"Mr Henshaw, you *will* do just as we say ..." She stopped speaking.

I could hear Dad's angry voice at the other end of the phone.

"Listen to me, Mr Henshaw," the woman told him. "I have someone here who'll make you change your mind. Say hello to your dad, Angela."

She thrust the phone at me.

"Dad ..." I said softly. "Dad, is that you?"

"Angela ...?" Dad was shocked. "Angela, are you OK?"

"Dad, I'm scared ..." The phone was yanked away from me.

"Time's up," said the woman. She and the blond man left the room. The woman was still talking into the phone as she went.

"Like I said, be a good girl and you'll soon be home," said Quill.

He left the room and locked the door behind him.

I made myself relax. The rope round my wrists felt a little loose. I lay down on the floor. I didn't make a sound. I lay on my side and tucked my knees under my chin. Then I slipped my tied hands past my hips and down the backs of my legs. Soon I was working away to free the rope that tied my ankles.

It cut into my fingers as I worked, but at last it fell away. It was not so easy to free my hands. I had to use my teeth and the finger of one hand and the thumb of the other to undo the knot. But I did it.

Now what?

I stood up and went over on tip-toe to the window. It was no good. There was no way that I could pull away the planks from over the window without making a lot of noise.

Think … think … think …

I looked in my pockets. I hoped that something in there would give me an idea. I looked around. My mind was still a blank. I tip-toed across to the door. Even though I knew

Quill had locked the door, I tried to open it. No good.

I peeked through the keyhole. Was there anyone outside? I couldn't see a thing because the key was in the lock.

That's when I had an idea. A very risky idea ...

I crept across the room to get the newspaper that was lying on the table. I laid it flat on the floor, then pushed it half under the door, so that it was under the key.

I had some gum and a safety pin in my pocket. I put the gum in my mouth, to make it soft. I unbent the safety pin and poked it into the lock. The key dropped out on the other side. It fell with a clink onto the newspaper.

Had my kidnappers heard anything?

I pulled the newspaper through to my side of the door. The key was lying on it. I froze. Would anyone come rushing up the stairs?

Silence.

I unlocked the door and opened it wide. I still had the gum in my mouth. The next part was very hard. I ran to the window and banged my fists on the planks.

"Help … HELP!" I yelled.

At once I heard footsteps coming up the stairs.

Please let it be all of them … I prayed.

I ran across the room and stood behind the door. I had the key in my hand.

"I thought you had tied her up," the woman said. She was angry.

"I did," Quill told her.

"The door's wide open," said the blond man.

They all rushed into the room. This was it. I ran around the door, pulled it shut behind me and locked them in with the key.

Chapter 5
The Chase

Only just in time. The doorknob shook as they tried to get out. I took the gum out of my mouth and stuffed it into the keyhole. Then I jammed the pencil I'd found in my pocket into the lock.

"Get out of the way. I've got a spare key," the woman said.

I smiled. I did not *know* that they had a spare key when I jammed the lock, I did it just in case. Now the spare key would not work because the gum and my pencil were in the lock.

"Angela, open this door. NOW!" yelled the blond man.

'Not on your life!' I thought. I ran down the stairs. I didn't have much time.

There it was – what I'd been looking for. *The phone* ...

The others were still shouting at me from the upstairs room.

I picked up the phone. Where would Dad be? At home or his shop? I didn't have time to find out. I had better phone the police. I dialled 999. "Police," I said.

Upstairs, my kidnappers were trying to batter the door down. At last I got through to the police.

"Please help me. My name's Angela Henshaw. My dad owns Henshaw's jewellery shop in the High Street. I've been kidnapped.

The kidnappers left Deansea by the Old Church Road. We drove on for about three minutes, then 600 left, 1,400 right, 120 right. No! Don't ask me what that means! Ask Dad. I've been kidnapped and I don't know where ..."

But at that moment, my kidnappers smashed the door down. I froze.

Then it all began to happen. There were shouts and then the sound of running footsteps. In a panic, I threw myself at the front door and yanked at the door latch.

'Don't turn around ...' I told myself over and over again.

The door opened.

"ANGELA ...!" my kidnappers shouted.

"COME BACK HERE ..." they called.

They were close.

'Don't turn around,' I told myself.

I felt a hand touch my back. I yelled and ran towards the moonlit trees as fast as I could.

I had to get away before that hand could get a good grip. Then the moon went behind a cloud and I couldn't see a thing. But I had to keep going to get away from my kidnappers.

"ANGELA, WE WON'T HARM YOU ..."

"DAMN IT! COME BACK ..."

Their voices seemed all around me.

'Don't look back, Angela,' I told myself. 'Keep running.'

I slipped, got up and kept on running until I couldn't hear the voices any more.

And then the ground fell away under my feet and I was falling and falling. I thought I'd never stop.

Chapter 6
Cliffhanger

I must have fainted. I woke up and thought at first I'd been having an awful dream.

But this was no dream. It was still dark and very cold and I was sore all over. I couldn't see a thing.

I felt around me with my hands. I was on this long, thin ledge and beyond that there was nothing.

I didn't feel brave any more.

"HELP!" I yelled at the top of my voice. "HELP!"

The ledge shook under me. Fear gripped me.

I felt behind me for a hand-hold. There was none. And I was so cold and so tired that I just wanted to sleep. But Dad had told me that you *must* keep awake if you are ever stuck outside in the cold. "If you go to sleep you might never wake up again," he had said.

Dad … If only I could see him one more time – just to hug him and say … sorry.

"HELP!" I yelled.

"ANGELA? ANGELA!"

And then there was a light shining in my eyes.

"Angela, hang on. I'm here with the police. You've fallen down a pit. Stay still. We're coming down to get you."

I started to cry again. It was Dad's voice.

Dad had come to get me.

In the light of the torch above, I saw a policeman tie a rope around his waist.

"Angela. It's all right. I'm coming to get you," said the policeman. "So don't run off, will you!"

That made me laugh a bit, but I was still crying too.

Dad and the other policemen and women then held on to the other end of the rope.

One policeman came down for me and lifted me onto his back. Then he pulled himself back up to the top of the pit with me.

Dad lifted me off the policeman's back. Dad hugged me and I hugged Dad. We were both crying. The police were standing around grinning at us.

"Dad, did you give the kidnappers your jewels?" I asked.

"Angela, I would have given them everything I had to have you safe and back home," Dad smiled.

"How did you know where to find me?" I sniffed.

"We got to your dad just as he left his shop with two bags filled with jewels for the kidnappers," said a policeman.

Dad and I smiled at each other.

"You should have told us sooner," said one policeman to Dad. "We know what to do when someone has been kidnapped."

"I didn't want to risk messing things up," Dad said. "Angela means more to me than all the jewels in the world."

"Where are the kidnappers?" I asked.

"We've got them all!" grinned a policewoman. "They still don't understand how you could have told us where you had been taken. You couldn't see anything with the scarf over your eyes."

"Why don't you both go off now. We can wait until tomorrow to ask you lots more questions," said one policeman.

"Can we go home?" I asked Dad.

"I'll cook you all the things you like best, beans, bangers and mash while you have a bath and get warm. Then we'll talk. OK?"

"OK," I grinned.

And we walked hand in hand back to Dad's car.

Our books are tested
for children and young people by
children and young people.

Thanks to everyone who consulted on
a manuscript for their time and effort in
helping us to make our books better
for our readers.

More *4u2read* titles...

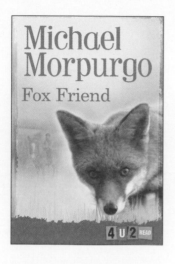

Fox Friend
MICHAEL MORPURGO

When Clare finds a fox cub that has got away from the hunt, she wants to keep him and make him well. But Clare's dad says foxes are bad.

How can Clare keep the cub safe?

Don't Go in the Cellar
JEREMY STRONG

What a silly thing to write!

"Don't Go in the Cellar."

It just makes people WANT to go in the cellar. People like Zack and Laura.

Now, if only they could find it...

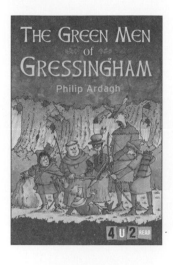

The Green Men of Gressingham

PHILIP ARDAGH

The Green Men are outlaws, living in a forest. Now they have taken Tom prisoner!

What do they want from him?

Who is their secret leader, Robyn-in-the-Hat?

And whose side should Tom be on?

The Red Dragons of Gressingham

PHILIP ARDAGH

The Green Men used to be outlaws. They lived in the forest and did brave deeds.

Now the Green Men are inlaws. They live in the forest and do... not very much.

The Green men are bored. They need some fun. They need a quest...

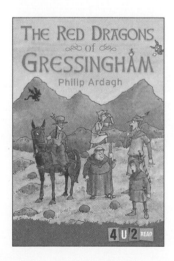

www.barringtonstoke.co.uk